Tru
Bl

Jeffrey Lee

True Blue

a novel

DELACORTE PRESS

Published by
Delacorte Press
an imprint of
Random House Children's Books
a division of Random House, Inc.
New York

Visit us on the Web! www.randomhouse.com/kids
Educators and librarians, for a variety of teaching tools, visit
us at www.randomhouse.com/teachers

Library of Congress Cataloging-in-Publication Data

Lee, Jeffrey.
True blue / Jeffrey Lee.
p. cm.
Summary: Molly's life was turned upside down by the car accident
that injured her and crippled her father, but at her new middle
school she teams up with a weird misfit for a science competition
and makes a true blue friend.
ISBN 0-385-73093-4 (trade)
[1. Abnormalities, Human–Fiction.   2. Schools–Fiction.
3. Science projects–Fiction.   4. People with disabilities–Fiction.
5. Fathers and daughters–Fiction.]   I. Title.
PZ7.L512525Tr 2003
[Fic]–dc21   2003002366

The text of this book is set in 11-point Baskerville Berthold.

Book design by Angela Carlino

Printed in the United States of America

September 2003

10   9   8   7   6   5   4   3   2   1

BVG

For Madeline and Juliana,
who give my words wings

ACKNOWLEDGMENTS

My deepest thanks to Joel, my fiercest ally; and to Marissa for encouraging and prodding in just the right proportions.

Thanks also to these people, who so generously gave their time and assistance along the way: Madeline Lee, Ryan Pearson, Kevin McNabb, Molly Tollefson, Mary Thompson, Sandy Monroe, Devan Wardrop-Saxton, Pearl Schwind, Jodie Wohl, Carey Hert, and Dorian Karchmar.

Prologue

He was trying to cheer me up.

We were driving home from my soccer game, and my team had just gotten creamed. Dad was goofing around, trying to make me laugh. I pretended to ignore him, but as usual, that just egged him on.

"Aha!" he said in his mad scientist voice. "Even now, zee diabolical laughing formula is racing through your veins. Vy do you even try to resist? Give in, my little cabbage . . . give in!"

I started cracking up. It was the "little cabbage"

thing that did it. When I knew I couldn't hold it in anymore, I bugged my eyes out and made a face at him. I knew that would get him.

He laughed. It was that big, booming laugh he used to have that made his whole body shake. He laughed so hard there were tears in his eyes.

I don't remember much after that.

1

"**Change is good**," said Mom. "It's a fresh start." She unwrapped another dish and put it up on the shelf.

"But I don't want a fresh start," I said. "I liked my old school."

"We can't afford your old school, Molly. You don't know how lucky we were to find an apartment in such a great school district. Families that could afford to send their kids anywhere send them to Pine Ridge Middle School. I hear they have a great soccer team."

"I don't care. I don't play soccer anymore." I

reached under the table and felt the long, bumpy scar on my knee.

"Well, maybe it's about time you started again. It's been more than a year."

I unwrapped a coffee mug and handed it to her.

"It won't be the same," I said. "I won't know anyone on the team."

Mom looked at me and sighed.

"You'll make new friends. I promise. Now stop complaining and make yourself useful. Weren't you going to make Dad's supper? Don't keep him waiting."

I got up and found the peanut butter and jelly and made a sandwich. Then I cut the sandwich up into little pieces and put them into the blender, poured in some milk, and turned it on. It made a thick, purple-gray milk shake. I poured it into a cup, put in a straw, and took it out into the front room.

Dad was sitting in his wheelchair in front of the TV.

"Peanut butter and jelly again," I said. I set up his tray and put the cup where he could reach the straw with his mouth. "Mom hasn't had time to go shopping yet. I think she's going after she unpacks the kitchen."

He nodded and stared at the TV. It was one of those game shows where people answer trivia questions to win money. Some guy had just won half a million dollars. He was jumping up and down and hugging a woman in a shiny dress. Dad watched with a blank expression on his face.

"Time for your exercises," said Mom. She came in holding a little mirror and a piece of paper. "Ellen said we have to do these every night. She says speech therapy once a week isn't enough—we have to work on your muscles in between her visits."

"Not . . . now," said Dad. His voice was slow and slurred, and he struggled with every syllable. The accident had happened more than a year before, but I could still barely understand him. He sounded as if he were talking underwater.

"*Yes*, now. Ellen's visits are expensive. I'm not going to let them go to waste."

She grabbed the remote and turned down the sound. Dad sighed.

"All right," said Mom, reading from the piece of

paper. "First we warm up with some stretches. Make a big smile."

Dad stared at her for a minute, then tried to smile. The muscles on the left side of his face moved okay, but the right side stayed still. His mouth opened up into a strange, twisty shape. It wasn't much of a smile.

"Good," said Mom. "Now watch yourself and try to make your right side move. If it starts to move, concentrate on making the movement bigger." She held up the mirror for him to see.

Dad tried to smile bigger, but that just opened his mouth wider and pulled it over to one side. He looked like the Hunchback of Notre Dame. He stopped and turned away.

"That was good, dear. Do you want to try again?"

He shook his head.

"No," he said. "No . . . more."

"Rick," said Mom, "Ellen really stressed how important this is."

"Ellen . . . is . . . an . . . id-i-ot," he said. He turned the sound up on the TV.

Mom just sat there. Her chin started shaking, and her eyes filled with tears.

"Fine," she said. She got up and pulled on her coat. "I'm going to the grocery store." She slammed the door behind her.

Dad stared at the TV. Some woman had just won a trip to Mexico. I got up and went to my room. I started school the next day.

Pine Ridge Middle School was only a few blocks from the new apartment. At my old school, there were only eighty kids in the whole building. Hundreds of kids were pouring into this school. I squeezed through the front door with everyone else and followed the signs to the office.

"May I help you?" the woman behind the front desk asked in a nasal voice. She smelled like perfume and cigarette smoke, and her bright orange hair matched her fingernails. It was a color you don't usually see, except on parrots. She wore it in a bun so tight it pulled back the skin around her eyes. The nameplate on her desk said MISS GRUBER.

"I'm new," I answered. "I'm supposed to be in Mrs. Raptor's first-period biology class."

"We'll see about that," she said.

She took out a little pair of glasses and perched them on her nose. "Name?"

"Molly O'Connor." She pulled some papers out of a drawer and ran a long orange fingernail down the first page. When she got to the bottom, she started on the next one. I sat down on a bench by the wall and stared at the ceiling.

After about a year, she looked up and smiled triumphantly.

"Here we are! O'Connor, Molly B. You should be in Mrs. Raptor's first-period biology class."

"Gee, thanks," I said.

"Wait here. Mr. Dinkerman will want to take you there himself. He does that for *all* the new students."

"Mr. Dinkerman?"

"Our principal. Wait right here."

She got up and knocked on the door at the back of the office. A short man in a dark blue suit answered. He was balding, but he had one of those hairdos where you grow the hair really long on one side and comb it over the top to cover it up. He walked over to me and held out his hand.

"Hello, Mary. I'm Mr. Dinkerman."

I shook his hand. It was soft and damp.

"Molly," I said.

"What?"

"Molly. My name is Molly."

He grinned, as if he'd meant it as a joke. "Yes, of course it is."

• • •

As we walked through the halls, Mr. Dinkerman's shiny black shoes squeaked on the linoleum.

"You're very lucky. We don't often get transfers in the middle of the year," he said. "In the fall, we have a waiting list. I'm sure you're aware we have quite a reputation."

He looked at me expectantly, so I nodded.

"Did you know that Congressman Jenkins sends his children here? We're all very proud of that. And quite a few of our parents work at TechnoSoft."

The more he talked, the slower he walked, and I was already late. The hallways were empty. Everyone else was in class.

"What do your parents do?" he asked.

I tried to walk faster.

"My mom works in a restaurant."

"How nice. We have another student whose family owns a French restaurant downtown. Chez Etienne, I think it's called. And what about your father?"

"Um . . . he's a writer."

"A writer! Wonderful! I don't believe any of our other parents are writers. Ah, here we are—Mrs. Raptor's room."

He opened the door and waved me into the room ahead of him. The teacher stopped in mid-sentence. All the kids turned and stared.

"Good morning, Mrs. Raptor, good morning, boys and girls. I have a new student who will be joining your class for the rest of the year. This is Mary O'Connor."

"Molly," I said. A few kids laughed.

"Yes, of course. As I was saying, Molly has just moved here. Her mother is in the restaurant business, and her father is a writer. I've been telling her what an exceptional school we have, and I'm sure she will fit in wonderfully."

Everyone was still staring. I looked down at the floor.

"Thank you, Mr. Dinkerman," said Mrs. Raptor. She was a small woman with bright, piercing eyes. "I'm sure you're right. We'll do everything we can to make Molly feel at home."

Mr. Dinkerman patted my shoulder with his big, clammy hand and left.

"Molly," said Mrs. Raptor, "please take a seat. I can meet with you after class to get you oriented. For now, just listen and try to catch whatever you can."

There were a few empty seats in the back corner. Only one kid was there, slumped down in his chair. I sat down next to him.

"As I was saying," said Mrs. Raptor, "the TechnoSoft Corporation is sponsoring a citywide science competition this year. No one is required to enter, but those who do will have class time to work on their projects and will be excused from some of our other work. You may choose a topic from any of the natural, physical, or technical sciences. Since a major goal of the competition is to encourage teamwork and cooperation, you must work in teams of two. Entry forms are due at the end of the month. Any questions?"

A large boy with dark, curly hair held up his hand.

"Yes, J.T.?"

He looked like he could be in high school. He grinned and glanced around before he spoke.

"What do I get when I win?"

Two girls in front of me giggled. They were both wearing tight sweaters and jeans. One of them had a long, shiny French braid, and the other had wavy blond hair down to her waist. They looked like a shampoo commercial.

"According to this," said Mrs. Raptor, "the ten finalists will each receive two hundred fifty dollars' worth of TechnoSoft software. The winners of the overall competition will receive Cybertron XL-4000 laptop computers and a selection of computer accessories."

"*My* laptop's twice that fast," the blond girl whispered to her friend. She turned and looked at me. Her mouth was smiling, but her eyes were giving me the once-over. When she got down to my shoes, she glanced at her friend and smirked. I pulled my feet under my desk. One of my shoes had a hole.

"We only have a few minutes left," said Mrs. Raptor. "I'm going to give you time to form teams and brainstorm ideas for the competition. You may quietly leave your seats and move about the room."

All the other kids got up and started pairing off. The only ones who stayed in our seats were me and the kid next to me. He kept peeking over at me, but he'd turn away the second I looked back at him. He was a strange-looking boy—much stranger than I had noticed when I first sat down.

His hair was very short and fine, just a layer of brown fuzz. His skin was dark and kind of shiny, but I couldn't tell if he was African American or Asian or what. His eyes were dark too—almost black, so you couldn't tell where his pupils started. Even his clothes were black: black sneakers, black pants, black T-shirt, and on top of it all a long black overcoat that was much too big for him.

"Hi," I finally said.

He looked at me.

His eyes got real big; then he turned his chair so I couldn't see his face.

I was late for every class. It was a big building, and I kept getting lost. I was even late for lunch, because I had to go to the office and ask Miss Gruber for lunch vouchers. "We don't have many students on the free lunch program," she said. First she had to find my name on another list, and then she had to find the vouchers. It took forever.

The serving ladies at the lunch line wore pink polyester tops with white collars and trim. They all had black hairnets and blue hair. The first one had a gold plastic name tag that read MRS. GRYWZINSKY. I'd never seen so many consonants in one name. I must have been smiling at it.

"Vat you are looking at? Vat is so funny? You zink I have funny name?"

"No! I don't. I just thought of something that made me laugh."

"Okay, Miss Funny-Brain. Stop laughing already and tell me vat you vant."

There wasn't much of a selection. Everything looked and smelled like they'd been keeping it warm for a long, long time. One pan had mashed potatoes with a cracked yellow crust on top. Another had some lumpy brown liquid that stuck to the sides of the pan like glue. There was some steamed broccoli that looked more gray than green, and then there was a pile of brown disks sitting in a pool of grease.

"What are those?" I asked.

She threw a disk on a plate and slapped down a spoonful of potatoes beside it.

"Wait," I said, "I just want to know what it is."

"Salisbury steak," she said. "You vant gravy?"

Before I could say no, she splattered the lumpy

brown liquid all over everything and put the plate on my tray. I picked it up and slid down the line. I handed the cashier lady one of my lunch vouchers. She looked me over, then took it and waved me through.

The lunchroom was noisy and packed. I walked around searching for an empty chair. When I finally found one, I put my tray down.

"Oh, I'm sorry, you can't sit there." It was the girl with the French braid.

"Why not?"

"That's Vanessa's seat."

"Who's Vanessa?"

The blond girl walked up and put her hand on the chair.

"*I'm* Vanessa. You're new, right?"

"Yeah. I'm Molly. I didn't know you had special seats."

"This is where Courtney and I *always* sit." She flashed her smile again. It seemed like she had way too many teeth. "Did you just move here?"

"Yeah," I said.

"Oh, that's great! Where's your new house?"

"Um . . . I live on Third Street."

"That's right near here," said Courtney. "Is it one of those big apartment buildings?"

"Uh . . . yeah."

"It must be great to live so close to school," said Vanessa. "You don't have too far to walk." She looked down at my shoes.

"Well . . . I guess I'd better find someplace to sit."

"Great!" she said. "It was great talking to you. Have a great lunch."

I glanced back at them as I walked away. They were laughing hysterically. Whatever the joke was, it must have been *great*.

I headed for an empty table in the far corner of the room. Well, it was nearly empty. The weird kid with the black overcoat was sitting there, facing the wall.

"Mind if I sit here?" I asked.

He jumped a little, like I'd startled him. He glanced at me for a second, then looked away. I sat down at the other end of the table.

I tried again. "I'm Molly O'Connor."

"Chrys," he said. I could barely hear him above the lunchroom noise. "Chrys Lepido."

"So how come you're sitting here all by yourself?" I asked.

He took a minute to answer.

"I like being alone."

"Hey, that's okay with me," I said. "If you wanted to be alone, you should have said so." I got up to leave.

"No," he said. "You can stay."

He hunched over his food, almost like he was hiding it. He had a big plastic bowl full of salad. It wasn't a normal salad, though. It had a lot of long, thin, dark green leaves, but they didn't look like lettuce; there was something that looked like clover and something else that looked like grass. There wasn't any salad dressing either. With the salad, he had a glass jar full of cloudy yellow liquid. That was it.

"You have an interesting name," I said. "Where'd it come from?"

He gave me that startled look again.

"What do you mean?" he asked.

"Lepido. I've never heard it before. Where is your family from?"

"Oh. I don't know."

So much for conversation. After that, we just ignored each other and ate our lunches until someone walked up behind Chrys.

"Hey, Freak-Boy, what's for lunch?" It was that big kid named J.T. from our class. He leaned forward with his hands on the back of Chrys's chair. "Big surprise! It's salad again. What are you, some kind of health nut? Every day you've got the same stupid salad. Don't you eat any *real* food?"

He reached down, grabbed a leaf out of Chrys's bowl, and popped it into his mouth. He chewed it for a second, then spat it out on the floor.

"*Blech!* That's nasty! Where'd you get that stuff, someone's yard?"

He reached for the bowl, but Chrys snatched it away and covered it with a lid. J.T. grabbed the glass jar instead.

"What's this?" He sniffed it, then put it down and jumped back. "I think it's dog piss. Hey, Lepido, you drinking dog piss?" He laughed a big, honking laugh, like a goose.

"Why don't you leave him alone?" I said. Up until then J.T. hadn't even noticed me sitting there. Chrys shot me a glance and shook his head.

"Hey, look," said J.T., smiling. "Lepido has a girlfriend!"

"What's your problem?" I said. "He isn't bothering you."

"No," said J.T. "But you are." He stopped smiling and took a step toward me.

"J.T.—good job." Mr. Dinkerman walked up and put his arm around J.T.'s shoulder. "I see you're already making friends with our new student."

"That's right, Mr. D. I was just letting her know how things work around here."

"That's terrific," said Mr. Dinkerman. "I knew I could count on you to make Mary feel welcome."

"My name is Molly," I said.

The bell rang for the end of lunch.

"Well, I guess you all need to get back to class."

"Sure thing, Mr. D.," said J.T. "Bye, Molly. Bye, Chrys. See you around." He smirked and walked away. Mr. Dinkerman walked off after him.

"Boy," I said, "what a jerk."

Chrys looked stunned. "Why'd you do that?"

"Do what?" I asked. "I just told him to leave you alone."

He screwed the cap onto the jar and stuffed it into his bag.

"You shouldn't have done that," he said. "It'll just make things worse." He picked up his things and hurried away.

"You're welcome," I said. "Really. Don't mention it."

4

"So how was it?" asked Mom. She was already in her waitress uniform when I got home.

"Okay."

"Okay? Is that all I get? How were your teachers? Your classes? The other kids?"

"Okay."

"Well, don't think I'm going to settle for 'Okay.' You can tell me all about it when I get home. There's some chili on the stove–it's been simmering all day. It should be soft enough for Dad. Don't forget your homework. I'll be home by ten-thirty."

"Wait, Mom, I need to ask you something."

"Molly, I'm already late. What is it?"

"Okay, it's fast. I just wanted to know if I can get some new shoes for school."

"New shoes? What's wrong with those?"

I showed her the hole.

She sighed. "We'll see. I'll think of something." She kissed me on the forehead and hurried out the door.

Dad was sitting in his wheelchair in the living room in front of the TV. I could hear him snoring. I tiptoed past him and spread my homework out on the kitchen table. Most of it was pretty easy. I had worked ahead a lot at my old school, so the math and the Spanish were a breeze. But the homework from Mrs. Raptor's class—that was something else.

In three pages or less, compare and contrast the main features that differentiate arthropod anatomy from our own. Draw a diagram to illustrate those differences.

After staring at a blank piece of paper for a while, I got up and dialed the phone.

"Hello, Hannah? It's me. Molly."

"Hey! How are you? It's so good to hear your voice. I kept meaning to call, but it's been crazy around here."

"That's okay," I said. "I've been busy too."

"I'll bet. How are you doing? How's your new school? Your new place?"

"They're okay."

"I'm sorry I didn't call. My grandparents were here over Christmas break, and it seemed like we were out doing something every day. Guess what? They got me a new stereo!"

"Wow," I said. "That's really nice of them."

"And it's crazy at school, too. We haven't even picked a new editor for the paper yet. I don't know *who* we could find to replace *you*."

I asked her about everyone we knew. I wanted her to tell me everything. I kept her on the phone a long time.

"I have to go finish my homework," she finally said. "I'll tell everyone you said hi."

"Yeah," I said. "I'll come visit soon."

"I hope so! It's hard to believe you aren't here anymore. We all miss you a lot."

"I miss you too."

A couple of hours later, I heard Dad coughing in the other room, so I went to check on him. He was tilted over to one side, and there was a big wet spot on his shirt from drool. I sat him up straight and wiped off his chin.

"Are you hungry? Mom made chili."

He nodded. I went into the kitchen, spooned out a bowl, brought it back to the living room, and set up his tray.

"It's kind of hot," I said. I scooped up a spoonful, blew on it, then tested it myself to make sure the beans were soft enough for Dad to chew. I put a little in his mouth. Then I fed myself. It took a long time to get through a whole bowl that way.

"How . . . was . . . sch . . . schoo . . . ?" he asked.

"School? It was okay."

"That . . . bad?"

"Yeah," I said. "It was pretty bad. It's really big, and the kids are all snooty."

"All?"

"Well, the ones I met. There's one kid who isn't, but he's totally weird."

Dad was about to say something else, but he started choking. I slapped him on the back, but he couldn't stop coughing. He threw up all over the tray.

I cleaned up the mess and got him into a clean shirt.

"Do you want some more chili?" I asked. "I could put it in the blender this time."

He closed his eyes and shook his head. I washed the dishes and went back to my homework.

5

"Okay, everyone," said Mrs. Raptor, "that's it for today. Don't forget to hand in your homework. And anyone who's decided to enter the science competition should let me know soon. The entry forms are on my desk."

As Chrys stood up, a page of his homework slid off his desk. I picked it up. It was a diagram comparing a wasp to a human being. The detail was unbelievable; there were hundreds of labels and little arrows. It was a work of art. Even the writing was beautiful.

"Wow. This is amazing."

Mrs. Raptor had walked up behind me. "As always, Chrys, you exceed expectations."

She took our homework and started to walk away, then stopped.

"Molly, I wanted to ask you something. I noticed that your father's name is Richard. Is he the Richard O'Connor who wrote the science column for the *Times*?"

"Uh . . . yeah. Why?"

"I used to read his column every week. But I haven't seen it in over a year–isn't he writing it anymore?"

"No, he's not. He . . . he's doing other stuff right now."

"Well, please tell him I'm a fan of his. I was wondering, do you think he might come in and talk to our class sometime? I'm sure he's a wonderful speaker. We could even put together an assembly for the whole school."

"Um . . . I don't know. He's pretty busy. . . ."

"Of course. But it wouldn't have to be anything formal. He could talk off the top of his head–just ramble on about anything that comes to mind. It would be fascinating. Would you ask him?"

"Uh . . . well, sure. I guess I could ask. . . ."

"Wonderful! I'll check the calendar and find a good day."

She walked away, humming to herself. I sighed. Chrys was standing there watching me with a puzzled look on his face.

"What?" I said.

"Nothing," he mumbled. He turned and walked away.

My first few days at Pine Ridge were all pretty much the same. I figured out where all the bathrooms were—that was a big highlight. Other than that, I went to classes and kept to myself. It was like being invisible. I ignored everyone and no one paid any attention to me. But that kid Chrys—he was hard to ignore.

Whatever else you thought about him, he was interesting. He came to school in the same clothes every day, and he wore that ratty old overcoat no matter how hot it was. He got up to go to the bathroom at least once every class, sometimes twice. When he raised his hand, you knew he needed to go, because he never raised his hand for anything else. It was a big joke. Everyone laughed at him.

Besides biology, I had two other classes with him—math and PE. He was good at math. I could see 100% written at the top whenever he got his homework back. I was the only one who sat near him in that class too.

In PE, he never joined in; he just sat in the corner reading a book. Once in a while J.T. would throw a ball at him or something, but Chrys would always just ignore it.

One day when the class was playing volleyball, I was excused too. I took out my journal and walked over to where he was sitting. He seemed kind of anxious about it, but I sat down anyway. I wanted to talk to him about an idea I had.

"How come you never do PE?" I asked.

"I'm excused," he said.

"I can see that. Why?"

"I've got a medical condition."

"Oh."

I glanced at his book. It was a thick textbook with lots of diagrams called *Aerodynamics and Flight*.

"How about you?" he asked, still staring at his book. I could barely hear him.

"I'm not supposed to play volleyball. Too much diving around and falling on your knees."

I showed him the scar on my knee. It's pretty impressive. It's about ten inches long and all bumpy and purple. He stared at it for a long time before he finally got up the nerve to look me in the eyes.

"I was in a car accident," I said. "About a year ago."

"Was it serious?"

"Yeah. I had to have an operation."

"That's too bad. Was anyone else hurt?"

I hesitated.

"My dad got hurt pretty bad."

"I'm sorry," he said. "Is he okay now?"

"No," I said. "Not yet."

That's all I told him, but it felt good to tell somebody *something*. After a few minutes, he went back to his book. The sleeves of his overcoat were rolled up, and for the first time I noticed how skinny he was. His arms and fingers were long and thin. They looked fragile, like little sticks.

"What's that book about?" I asked.

"It's about air movement and how it affects things when they fly."

"Are you into that stuff?"

"Yeah. Kind of." He closed the book and put it facedown on the floor. "What about you? What are you reading?"

"I'm not reading–I'm writing. In my journal."

"What do you write?"

"Lots of stuff," I said. "Whatever I'm thinking about. It's kind of private."

"That's okay," he said. "I'm kind of private, too. But I like your writing. Like that essay you wrote–the one Mrs. Raptor read in class. You're a good writer."

"Thanks."

"Your dad must be proud of you." He went back to reading his book.

● ● ●

When PE was over, we both got up to go.

"Hey, I wanted to ask you something," I said. "I

had this idea. You're good at science and drawing, and I'm pretty good at putting things into words. You know the science competition? I'll bet we'd make a good team. Maybe we could show these snooty kids a thing or two. What do you think?"

He had a startled look on his face.

"Chrys? Did you hear me?"

"Yeah. The science competition. Teaming up . . . and stuff."

"Right. So? What do you think?"

"Um . . . sure. Why not?"

For the first time since I'd met him, he smiled. He had a nice smile. It made his whole face look different. Then he started to blush.

"Okay," he said. "I've got to go to class. We'll talk some more later . . . about the competition, I mean. Okay, bye."

He hurried out of the gym.

I looked down and noticed that he'd left his book. When I leaned over to pick it up, I saw something strange. On the gym floor, next to the wall where he'd been leaning, was a thin film of dust. I ran my finger through it and held it up to the light. It was a shiny blue powder made of tiny flat specks.

They looked like little diamonds when I moved them under the light.

I leaned down and blew across the floor. The dust swirled up in a little sparkling cloud. Then it was gone.

7

That night, Mom looked tired when she got home.

"Hi," I said. "Long day?"

She plopped down in a chair at the kitchen table and kicked off her shoes.

"The usual," she said. "I think some people go to restaurants just so they can treat their waitress like a slave. How about you? How was your day?" She reached down and rubbed her feet.

"Okay."

"Again with the *'Okay'*? Honestly, Molly, you'd

think I was asking you to reveal your deepest, darkest secrets. I just want to know how your day went."

"Well, what do you want me to say? It wasn't great, and it wasn't terrible. It was just like your day–the usual."

"Fine," she said. "I'm too tired to argue." She stretched out her legs and tilted back her head, then closed her eyes.

"Hey, Mom, tomorrow's Saturday. Can we go shopping for new shoes?"

"Actually," she said, "that reminds me. I picked something up on my way to work today."

She walked into the hall and came back with my shoes. Then she reached into her purse and pulled out something that looked like a big tooth-paste tube.

"What's that?" I asked.

"It's called Shoe-Renew. Just watch."

She took the cap off and squeezed some thick, brown goop onto the bottom of my shoe. It smelled awful–like something you'd use to clean your oven. She spread it around with her finger and filled in the hole.

"There," she said. "It'll dry by morning. Good as new!"

"Good as new? Mom, it looks like dog poop!"

"Shoes are expensive, Molly. We can't throw away a perfectly good pair just because it offends your fashion sense."

"But Mom . . ."

"Forget it, Molly. End of discussion. Now go brush your teeth. It's bedtime."

I stomped out of the kitchen. On my way to the bathroom, I passed Dad in his wheelchair. He glanced up at me, his face all pale and blue in the TV light. He looked so sad.

"Okay, settle down," said Mrs. Raptor. "I have a little surprise for you today."

She walked around the room handing out copies of an old newspaper article.

"This is an article that relates to our next unit on the human body. It's about how the things we do every day can affect our hearts. I'd like everyone to note that the article was written by Molly's father."

Everyone turned around and looked at me.

"Molly has asked her father to come in and talk to us someday. He can tell us all about how he became a science writer. I was hoping he might also help pick our school's first-round winners in the science competition, but it turns out Molly and Chrys have decided to enter as a team. That obviously disqualifies Mr. O'Connor as a judge."

Vanessa and Courtney looked back and forth between Chrys and me and started whispering and giggling.

"Quiet down," said Mrs. Raptor. "Everyone take a few minutes to read the article, and then we'll discuss it. However, those of you who have entered the science competition may move to the library to work on your projects."

As Chrys and I gathered up our stuff, Vanessa turned around again and grinned. Chrys hurried out the door.

"You guys will make a *great* team," she said to me.

I could see Courtney behind her, trying not to laugh.

"I think we'll do okay," I said.

"I'm sure you will," said Vanessa. "You guys were made for each other."

●　　●　　●

When we got to the library, I slammed my notebook down on a table. Chrys looked at me.

"What?" I said, glaring back.

"Are you mad at me?" he asked.

"No—I'm not mad at you. It's those jerks."

"What did they say to you?"

"They said . . . nothing. Never mind. It doesn't matter. I'm just sick of them. How can you stand them? You get it even worse than I do. How can you just sit there and take it?"

Chrys shrugged. "I figure the less I say, the less they'll notice me."

"Well, I'm not as good as you at keeping my mouth shut. I can't believe I told Mrs. Raptor my dad would come and talk. I'm such an idiot."

"You don't think he'll come?"

"Are you kidding? He doesn't even leave the apartment, never mind talk to anyone."

"How come?"

"He's in a wheelchair, and his voice is all messed up from the accident. He can't move the muscles in his throat, and he can't really swallow. It sounds like he's gargling instead of talking. Most people can't even understand him."

"Can *you*?"

"Yeah, mostly. But it's hard. Anyway, it doesn't matter—he doesn't talk to me much either."

"How come?"

Because it's my fault, I thought. But I didn't say that.

"I don't know. Mostly he sits in front of the TV. It's weird. Before the accident, he *never* watched TV. He always said it'd turn your brain into Cream of Wheat. He mostly spent his time writing."

"Does he still write?"

"No. His right arm doesn't work, and his left arm was broken in a bunch of places. He can move it, but not very far. He used to write on a big old manual typewriter. He said he loved pounding words into paper. Now he can't even press the keys down."

"So he can't work?"

"No. My mom works instead."

Chrys didn't say anything for a while. Finally he opened his notebook and took out a pencil.

"So, what should we do for our project?" he asked.

"I don't know. I thought we could just brainstorm for a while and come up with a few ideas."

Chrys made a big, toothy smile and tossed his head, as if he were flipping back a bunch of long hair.

"*Great!* That's a *great* idea! I'm sure we'll think of something *great*!" he said in a whiny, high-pitched voice.

It was a perfect imitation of Vanessa. We both started laughing. The librarian shushed us, but that just made us laugh harder.

9

It took us a while to decide what to do for a project. Chrys's wasp diagram was no fluke; he was good at biology. His specialty was insects. He knew tons of stuff about them—stuff you couldn't just look up in a textbook or an encyclopedia. But every time I thought of a way we could use that, he didn't want to do it.

"Why can't we do something about humans?" he said.

"Humans are boring," I said. "Besides, we're doing human physiology in class. Everyone will know about that stuff. We need something different—something with a little piz-zazz."

"But why insects?"

"Because they're cool. Some of them are so beautiful, up close, but some are like mutant alien monsters. Besides, you're already an expert. That'll give us a big advantage."

I convinced him. We decided to do a project on the life cycle of the butterfly. We'd build a giant model of each stage in the butterfly's life: egg, larva, pupa, and adult. Then we'd write an oral presenta-tion to go along with it.

We started out doing the project at school, but soon we realized we needed more time to work on it if we wanted to do it right—and win.

"Why don't we work on it this weekend?" I asked Chrys one day.

"Sure. Should we do it at your place?"

"It's kind of small," I said. "We'd have to work at the kitchen table, and we couldn't leave things out overnight."

"Well . . . I guess we could do it at my house."

"You don't sound so sure."

"It's probably okay," he said. "It's just my parents. They're kind of weird."

"Of course they are! They're parents."

"Yeah, I guess you're right. Okay, how about Saturday morning around ten?"

"Perfect. I'll be there."

● ● ●

On Saturday, I walked to the address Chrys had given me, carrying a box full of paper, glue, and paint. I'd also found some cool stuff in my apartment building's Dumpster that I thought might be useful. By the time I got there, the box was feeling pretty heavy.

Chrys lived at the end of a quiet street in an old house mostly hidden by bushes and trees. A tall wooden fence kept the backyard out of sight. I walked up the steps and rang the doorbell. A thin, nervous woman opened the door.

"Why, hello! You must be Molly." Her hands fluttered when she talked. "Chrys said you'd be coming around ten. And here it is, ten o'clock. And here you are, right on time."

She stood there smiling at me, her hands still flitting around.

"Hi," I said. "It's nice to meet you." I peeked at her over the top of the box, wobbling a little from the weight of it.

"Oh, what am I thinking? That must be heavy. Can I help you carry it?"

"No, that's okay. Maybe you could just show me where to put it down."

She led me up the stairs to a door at the end of the hall. She hesitated, then knocked.

"Chrys, dear? Your friend Molly is here. Are you ready for visitors?"

Chrys opened the door. He was wearing the same clothes as always, overcoat and all.

"Hey, Molly. Come on in."

He grabbed my arm and pulled me inside.

"Thanks, Mom," he said. "We'll just work in here."

"Well, all right, dear. But let me know if you need anything, okay? And don't open those windows so wide. It gets drafty up here."

"Okay, Mom."

He closed the door, leaned back against it, and rolled his eyes.

"I told you," he said.

"She's nice," I said. "Just a little nervous."

"She worries about me too much," he said.

I put the box down on the floor and looked around. Chrys's room was big, with lots of windows, all of them wide open. One wall was covered with bookshelves, and most of them were full. There were a small desk and a computer in one corner and a stepladder in another. Something about the room seemed strange, but I couldn't figure out what it was.

I walked to the window and looked out into the backyard. It was completely covered with garden beds. But it wasn't an ordinary garden. In every bed, there was only one thing growing—low, bushy plants with long, thin leaves.

"Look," said Chrys, "I already started."

I turned around. He pointed to a strange object on the floor. It was about two feet long and shaped like a stubby carrot. I picked it up. It was made of coat-hanger wire that was bent and twisted into a frame. A nylon stocking was stretched over the frame like a skin.

"I don't get it," I said.

"Here, I'll show you."

He picked up a little stuffed animal—a black cat that he had sewn some bright orange cloth on to look like wings. He folded up the wings and legs and stuffed it through the open end of the stocking and into the frame. Then he put a knot in the extra stocking material and let the whole thing dangle from the loose end.

"Oh my God," I said. "It's a cocoon!"

"Yeah. Or a chrysalis, if it's a butterfly. You like it?"

"It's brilliant!"

We got a start on the other models. For the eggs, we took tennis balls and covered them in plastic wrap. We started making the adult butterfly from more coat-hanger wire and one of Mrs. Lepido's old silk scarves. But my favorite was the caterpillar. We made a frame for the body from a piece of clothes-dryer duct I'd found in the trash, and cut up an egg carton for legs.

"We should put the first layer of papier-mâché on today," said Chrys. "It takes a long time to dry, and we're going to need two or three layers."

"I have to get home for dinner soon."

"Maybe you could eat dinner here," he said. "We could work on it afterwards."

"Do you think your parents would mind?"

"I don't know. I'll ask."

Chrys went downstairs to talk to his mother. He was gone for a while, but he came back smiling.

"She said yes. I had to convince her, though. She's always afraid I'll get tired or stressed out or something."

"Because of your . . . condition?"

"Yeah."

"So what did you tell her?"

"I told her you don't stress me out. I told her we're fine."

"Thanks for letting me stay for dinner," I said. "I hope it's not too much trouble."

"Of course not," said Mr. Lepido. He poured some water into my glass. "It's our pleasure."

"And I hope you don't mind us working on our project here. My apartment is pretty small, and . . ."

"Oh no, don't be silly," said Mrs. Lepido. "We love having you here."

"But when we start writing our presentation, we could do it at my place," I said. "We won't need so much room then."

Chrys's mother looked worried.

"Actually," she said, "wouldn't you both be more comfortable working here? Chrys gets so tired after the long week at school. . . ."

"Marion, what are you so worried about?" Mr. Lepido sounded annoyed. "He's just going over to a friend's house—not running a marathon."

"I know that," she said. "I'm just thinking of what's best for Chrys."

"Well, so am I."

There was an awkward silence. I glanced at Chrys. He was fidgeting in his chair.

"You know what?" I said. "We probably *would* be more comfortable here. That way, we can just keep working without moving our stuff. I don't mind coming over. Really."

"Well," said Mrs. Lepido, "that's very kind of you, Molly. As I said, we'd love to have you back anytime."

Mr. Lepido passed me a platter of food. "I hope you like meat loaf."

I took some, then tried to hand the platter to Chrys, but his mother intercepted it.

"Chrys is on a special diet," she said. "He has a sensitive stomach."

Instead of meat loaf and mashed potatoes, Chrys had a big helping of salad just like the ones he always ate at school. And instead of water, like the rest of us, he had a glass of that strange yellow liquid.

"I've been wondering," I said. "What exactly *do* you eat, anyway?"

Chrys picked up one of the long, thin leaves.

"This is milkweed," he said. "The rest is just clover, and a little grass."

"I thought you were supposed to have a *sensitive* stomach. *My* stomach couldn't handle that."

Chrys laughed and held up his glass.

"And this is nectar," he said.

"Nectar?"

"That's just what we call it," said his father. "It's a mixture of fruit juices, honey, protein powder, and a little Gatorade. Chrys has been drinking it since he was a baby. He can't digest milk."

"Can I try some?" I asked.

Chrys looked surprised. "Really?"

"Sure. Why not?"

He handed me his glass, and I took a sip. It was sweet, but not like I had expected. It smelled like roses.

"Wow," I said. "It's really good."

Chrys smiled.

●　　●　　●

After dinner, we went back up to work on our project. We tore strips of newspaper and dipped them in a paste made of flour and water. Then we spread the wet strips on top of the caterpillar frame to give it a kind of skin.

"You know what's funny?" said Chrys.

"What?"

"The way you act like everything I do is just normal."

I thought about that for a minute.

"Well, at first I thought you were pretty weird. But then, after I got to know you, it turned out you weren't."

"But how do you know?" asked Chrys. "How do you know I'm *really* normal?"

"No one's *really* normal," I said. "That's why *you're* just as normal as anyone else."

"Oh," said Chrys. He didn't sound convinced.

"This is really taking shape," I said. I put on another strip of paper and smoothed it down. "We should keep it somewhere safe so no one steps on it while it dries."

I looked around for a place to put it. That's when I figured out what was strange about Chrys's room.

"Hey, isn't this your bedroom?"

"Yes. Why?"

"Where's your bed?"

"Well . . . actually . . . I don't have a bed."

"Then where do you sleep?"

He hesitated.

"If I show you," he said, "do you promise you won't laugh?"

"Promise."

He walked to his closet and took out something that looked like a big rolled-up quilt. When he unrolled it, it turned out to be a kind of sleeping bag. Someone had gone to a lot of trouble to make it really strong. It was covered on the outside with heavy cloth and a bunch of crisscrossing straps.

Chrys got on the stepladder and hung the bag from a big metal hook in the ceiling. He climbed a few steps higher and slipped into the bag feetfirst.

His whole body disappeared, except for his face peeking out the top.

"I can't sleep lying down," he said. "I get all cramped up. Pretty strange, huh?"

"Wow," I said. "That is so cool."

"Really? You don't think it's weird?"

"Of course it's weird," I said. "But it's still cool."

11

For the next few weeks, we worked at Chrys's house whenever we could. It was going well. The models were nearly done, and they were coming out even better than I'd expected. That was mostly because of Chrys.

He had an incredible eye for detail. Nothing was too small for him to notice. He'd stare at a model for minutes at a time; then he'd change just one small thing. Little by little, he kept making them better. After a while, they were so good you could have put them in a science museum.

But then it was time to write the oral presentation. That was my specialty. Chrys had some good ideas, but it was my job to turn them into something interesting we could say.

One day, while we were working in the library, Chrys seemed kind of fidgety. He kept tapping his pencil and bouncing his heels on the floor.

"Would you stop that?" I said. "You're shaking the desk. Everything I write is coming out wobbly."

"Sorry," he said. "I'm feeling kind of cooped up. Couldn't we work outside?"

I looked around, but we weren't near any windows. "It was cloudy when I walked to school. It might be raining now."

"It's not. It's sunny and warm."

"How do you know?" I asked.

"I just do."

He was right. After we got permission from Mrs. Raptor, we went outside, and it was so warm I rolled up my sleeves. We could hear a lawn mower somewhere nearby, and the air smelled like fresh-cut grass. We sat on the blacktop and leaned against a wall. The bricks were warm against our backs. Chrys kept his coat on anyway, but he seemed much happier with his face in the sun, until someone walked up and blocked it. It was J.T.

"Hey, look," he said. "It's the two little love-birds."

"What are *you* doing here?" I said. "You're supposed to be in class."

"So are you," he said.

"We're doing our science project."

"Hey," he said, "I am too. I'm studying the mating habits of freaks and geeks."

"Oh," I said, "is it your mating season already?"

"You know what, O'Connor? You've got a big mouth. The only reason I haven't shut you up is because you're a girl. Of course, that won't help your little boyfriend here. Maybe I'll teach *him* a lesson instead."

Chrys's eyes got big. He hugged his knees and shrank against the wall.

"Leave him alone," I said, getting up. "You want to hit someone? Hit *me*. I'll make sure they kick you out of school."

"Oh yeah? And who's gonna do *that*? You ever hear of Congressman Jenkins? That's my father. Dinkerman thinks he's God. Oh, but I forgot—*your* daddy is a famous writer. So famous they canceled his stupid newspaper column."

"Shut up," I said.

"No wonder they got rid of him. I read that article Raptor handed out. It sucked. Your dad writes like a retard."

Something inside me snapped. I don't know what happened. I must have tried to tackle him or something. Whatever I did, it wasn't too smart. He was stronger than me. He locked my head under his arm and wouldn't let go.

"Hey, Freak-Boy! I'm dancing with your girlfriend. Aren't you going to rescue her? What's the matter? Scared?"

J.T. spun me around, and I caught a glimpse of Chrys. He looked terrified.

J.T. spun me around again, and all of a sudden I was looking down at a pair of bright red high-heeled shoes. J.T. let go. When I stood up, Miss Gruber was giving us the evil eye.

"Hey, Miss Gruber," said J.T. "We were just joking around. . . ."

"Save it," she said. "I don't know what you were doing, and I don't care. But you'd better have permission to be out here."

Chrys and I showed her the passes we'd gotten from Mrs. Raptor.

"How about you, Julius Theodore? Where's your pass?"

"Uh, I guess I must have lost it."

"That's fine," said Miss Gruber. "Because after I take a little break, I'm going back inside, and I'm going to walk by your class. I can tell Mrs. Raptor you lost her permission slip and ask her for another one. How does that sound?"

"You don't have to do that," said J.T. "I was just on my way back to class anyway."

"Yes," said Miss Gruber. "You looked like you were in quite a hurry."

Her eyes followed him back into the building. Then she wobbled across the playground on her high heels, all the way to the far side of the parking lot. She pulled out a cigarette and lit it.

"Hey," said Chrys, "are you all right?"

"Yes, no thanks to *you*," I said. I rubbed my neck.

"What did you want *me* to do? I'm half his size."

"And what am I, a giant? Listen, you don't have to rescue me—I can take care of myself. But how can you sit there and do nothing while he talks to you like that? Don't you have any self-respect? Do you *like* being the class freak?"

As soon as I said it, I wanted to take it back. Chrys just stared at me as tears welled in his eyes. He got up and walked away.

"Chrys!" I yelled after him. "I'm sorry! Please come back. I didn't mean that."

He started to run. He went right past the door and kept going. When he reached the end of the building, he rounded the corner and disappeared. I thought about going after him, but I didn't think it would do any good.

After he left, I stood there for a long time. I started crying, and once I started, I couldn't stop. Tears kept pouring out of me, and my whole body was shaking. I hadn't cried like that in a long time.

When I finally slowed down, I opened my eyes, and there were Miss Gruber's shoes again.

"Rough day, huh?"

I sniffed and nodded. She reached into her pocket and pulled out a handkerchief. She held it out for me with her long fingernails. Today they were bright red.

"Wanna talk about it?"

I shook my head and blew my nose. Her hand-kerchief smelled like cigarettes.

"You wouldn't understand."

"You'd be surprised," she said. "You think you're the only one who ever felt like a weirdo? What do you think I was at your age, homecoming queen?"

"I don't want to be queen of anything. I just want things to go back to the way they were."

"Well," she said, "as soon as you figure out how to make time go backwards, let me know. Until then, you're better off letting it do what it does best."

"What's that?" I asked.

"Go forward. Sooner or later, even the worst day is over. The sun goes down, you go to sleep, and you try again tomorrow."

"Great," I said. "Life sucks—and then you get more."

She raised an eyebrow and stared at me.

"Hey, it's the only game in town. If you're lucky, you wake up and God gives you a brand-new day. After that, it's up to you. Life isn't easy. So what? Get over it."

She smiled, reached for my hand, and helped me to my feet.

"Watch the nails, honey," she said. "I just had them done."

I tried to give her handkerchief back, but she waved it away.

"You keep it, honey. Believe me, I've got plenty more where that came from."

"Thanks," I said.

"Don't mention it. Now let's go in before we *both* get busted."

She wobbled back inside ahead of me.

12

Chrys wasn't at school for the rest of the day. He wasn't at lunch, or in PE, or even in the halls. When the last bell rang, I ran straight to his house.

Mrs. Lepido answered the door. She looked even more nervous than usual.

"Molly, I'm so glad it's you. There's something wrong with Chrys—he came home early from school. He says he isn't sick, but he won't tell me what's wrong. Do you know? Did anything . . . out of the ordinary happen today?"

"Um, I'm not sure. I mean, I think something

upset him, but it was just a mistake. Can I talk to him?"

"He's locked in his room. He won't come out. He won't even answer me. Maybe he'll talk to you, Molly. I just don't know what to do."

I went upstairs and knocked on his door.

"Chrys? It's me, Molly. I need to talk to you. Chrys?"

I put my ear to the door. Nothing. Then something caught my eye. The door next to Chrys's was open, and up on the wall, a patch of faint blue light appeared, then vanished. It was only there a second, but it almost seemed to ripple, the way sunlight does when it shines on a pond. A minute later it came back, then disappeared again.

I went to get a closer look. The light on the wall was shining in through an open window, and when I leaned out, I saw where it was coming from. Just beyond the corner of the house, a shimmer of blue waved in and out of view.

I carefully climbed out the window onto the gutter and edged along the outside wall. When I got to the corner, I grabbed the drainpipe and leaned out so I could see.

Chrys was sitting on the roof, holding a jar of nectar. His overcoat was rolled up beside him, and his black T-shirt had two long rips down the back. Out of those rips, sweeping back like the sails on a ship, were two gigantic blue butterfly wings.

At first I thought it was some kind of costume. The wings shimmered in the sunlight, and the wind made them ripple like cloth. But as they opened and closed, I could see where they attached to his body. They moved with the muscles and the bones of his shoulders, and where they joined his back, they disappeared into his skin. I lost my grip.

My feet began to slip, and I started to slide down the roof. I think I yelled, or at least I tried to. I heard a flapping sound, a rush of air, and a scramble of feet. Then, just before I went over the edge, someone grabbed my wrist and pulled me back.

I looked up and saw Chrys's face, with his blue wings shimmering behind him. With one hand, he pulled me to my feet. I couldn't believe how strong he was.

We were both shaking. For a long time, we just stared at each other. Then he turned away and went back to his place on the roof. I crept after him and sat down a few feet away.

"What are you doing here?" he asked.

"I came to check on you. I was worried when you didn't come back to school. I wanted to apologize for being such a jerk and for calling you . . . you know . . . a freak."

"Well, I guess you don't have to apologize anymore. You were right."

I couldn't concentrate on what he was saying because I kept staring at those wings. They were about three feet long, and they seemed to change color—from blue to purple and back again—as they opened and closed in the sunlight.

"Why . . . why didn't you tell me?" I asked.

"Tell you what? *Hey, Molly, by the way, I'm actually a mutant insect thing. That* would have been a good conversation."

"I'm serious. You could've told me."

"Yeah, right. Since you're Miss Sensitive and all. Who are you kidding?"

"Okay," I said, "*now* who's being a jerk? I said I was sorry. What do you want?"

"Nothing. Just leave me alone."

I looked off into the distance and tried to think of something to say.

"Okay," I said. "If I'm just like the rest of them, why would I even be here?"

I waited a long time for an answer, but I didn't get one. As I got up to go, Chrys finally spoke.

"I don't know," he said. "Maybe you came to throw yourself off the roof so I'd have to save you."

"I slipped!" I said. "I nearly got killed! And it would have been your fault, too. I wouldn't even be up here if it weren't for you."

Chrys's shoulders started to shake, sending little ripples through his wings.

"You're welcome," he said. "Really. Don't mention it."

"You're laughing at me, aren't you?" I said.

"Who, me?" He tried to stop, but he couldn't. A laugh escaped through his nose with a snort.

"What was *that*?" I said. "Don't tell me you're part *pig,* too."

We both lost it. I laughed so hard I had to sit down so I wouldn't slip again. When I finally got control of myself, I slid down next to him.

"I really am sorry, you know."

"I know," he said. "It's not your fault. You didn't know I really *am* a freak."

"Don't say that," I said.

"Why not? It's true. What do *you* think I am?"

"Well . . . I guess I'm not sure. Maybe you can tell me."

"I wish I could," he said. "I wish *somebody* could. I'm kind of a medical mystery. I've seen a gazillion doctors since I was born. They just stare at me and scratch their heads."

"You were born this way?"

"Yeah. When I came out, it was kind of a shock for my parents. I think they're still trying to recover."

"But . . . but how? I mean, I've never heard of anything like this."

"Neither has anyone else. Some of the doctors wanted to write me up in the medical journals, but my parents wouldn't let them. They didn't want me to be a freak show."

"And none of them could help you? The doctors, I mean?"

"No. I'm just as weird inside as I am outside. They can't take these things off without messing up my other organs. It's too risky."

"Wow," I said. "When you said you had a medical condition, I thought it was asthma or something. But I guess this explains a lot."

"You mean my food? And my bed?"

"Yeah. And that funky old coat of yours. How do you keep them inside it, anyway? They don't look like they'd fit."

"It isn't easy," he said. "I have to fold them pretty tight. If I don't stretch them out once in a while, they start to cramp up and shake."

"Is that why you're always going to the bathroom at school?"

"Yeah."

I snuck another peek at his wings. They opened and closed slowly and glistened in the light. They were beautiful. Really strange, but beautiful.

"Well," he said, "what are you going to do?"

"What do you mean?" I said.

"Now that you know, what are you going to do?"

"I won't tell anyone. Not if you don't want me to."

"Actually, I was wondering if we were still going to be friends."

"Yeah," I said. "Of course. You have to stick by your friends, right?"

"I don't know," he said. "I never had any."

"You do now," I said.

He turned and looked at me.

"Yeah," he said. "I guess I do."

"And if you don't want to lose me, you should get me off this roof. I've nearly died twice in the last five minutes."

"Don't be so dramatic. If you stay still for a while, you'll get used to it."

"Why would I *want* to get used to it? What are you doing up here, anyway?"

He looked at me, trying to decide how to answer. Then he picked up the jar of nectar and held it out in front of him.

"Okay," he said, "I'll show you. Try not to move. And if you have to say something, say it softly. If you scare them, they won't come back for hours."

"Who won't? What are you talking about?"

"Shhh. Just watch."

He sat there, very still. He hardly even blinked. At first, nothing happened. I watched, waiting and wondering what on earth he was trying to do.

A small white butterfly drifted up from the edge of the roof and fluttered around our heads. Then a yellow one appeared, and two orange ones with black streaks on their wings. Some of them landed on the rim of the jar to sip the nectar, and others on Chrys's shoulders and hands. And they kept on coming.

Soon dozens of butterflies in all different shapes and colors were circling us and landing on us both.

"Oh my God," I whispered. "This is unbelievable. How do you do this?"

"I'm not sure," he said. "At first, it was just one or two at a time, but the more I came out here, the more there were. Now I can do it almost anywhere. But I don't like to do it when people are watching."

"I still don't get it. What do you do to *make* them come?"

"Nothing," he said. "Once they get here, they like the nectar, but all I do is sit and wait."

"You must be doing *something*," I said.

He shrugged.

"Sometimes nothing is the best thing to do."

13

It was the day of the science competition. Only one team would be picked to represent our school in the final round. We hurried to the gym after our last class to set up our presentation.

When we got there, everyone was busy getting ready. You could feel how nervous we all were; the air was practically tingling. Chrys and I found an empty table and started setting up our models. Vanessa walked by and stopped to look at them.

"Great worm!"

"It's not a worm," I said. "It's a caterpillar."

"Oh," she said. "Well, it looks *great,* whatever it is."

We barely had time to get everything ready before the judges started making their rounds. They were the four science teachers, including Mrs. Raptor, and Mr. Dinkerman made five. Chrys was too nervous to check out the other presentations; he wanted to practice ours. But I was curious. I went over and joined the crowd that was following the judges around the room.

We stopped at each team's table to hear their presentation. The competition looked pretty tough. Most of the teams had put in a lot of work. But when we got to Vanessa and Courtney, all they had on their table was a big plaster lump covered with burnt toothpicks and ashes. It smelled like an ashtray. It was supposed to be a replica of Mount St. Helens. Courtney said the toothpicks were "the charred ruminants of the ancient old-growth forest." I think she meant charred remnants, but the whole thing did kind of look like a burnt cow.

When they got to their demonstration, Vanessa poured a bunch of chemicals into a hole at the top of the lump. I'd seen people make volcanoes with baking soda and vinegar before, but this was different. There were lots of ingredients, and some of them smelled awful.

A little bit of smoke came out of the top, but that was it, so she poured in some more chemicals. Still nothing. Finally, she poured in everything she had, and shook the lump around to mix it up. I glanced over my shoulder to see how Chrys was doing, and that's when it happened.

BOOOOOM!

People were yelling and running around with their faces in their hands. There was smoke everywhere, and the whole gym smelled like rotten eggs.

Courtney was hysterical. Even after everyone else stopped screaming, she was still at it. But the center of attention was Vanessa. She was the one closest to the volcano lump when it blew. She was sitting on the floor, looking stunned, coughing and choking, with little chunks of plaster in her shampoo-commercial hair.

In the middle of all the craziness, I heard a strange noise coming from over by our table. I ran there and found Chrys on the floor, clutching his stomach. At first I thought he was hurt, but then I realized he was just laughing. When he finally calmed down, he looked up at me with a big smile and imitated Vanessa's voice:

"That was *great*!"

●   ●   ●

It took about half an hour to get everything cleaned up. Mrs. Raptor had to take Courtney outside to calm her down, and they took Vanessa off to the hospital, just in case. She looked okay, though. She was making calls on her cell phone as they wheeled her out.

I think all the crazy stuff helped us in the end. When our turn came, I wasn't nervous anymore. Chrys mumbled a little, but other than that, he was fine. And we must have done something right.

They gave us first place.

14

When I got home, Dad was working with Ellen, his speech therapist.

"Come on, Mr. O'Connor. Let's see that handsome smile."

She held a mirror up to Dad's face. His mouth twisted open.

"That's wonderful!" said Ellen. "Just like a movie star."

Dad grunted and started to cough.

"Now, what did I tell you, Mr. O'Connor? When you feel your saliva building up like that, you have to let some of it run out. If you try to swallow too much at once, you'll choke. A little mess on your chin is better than breathing it into your lungs. You'll give yourself pneumonia."

"I . . . won't . . . drool."

"Oh, don't be so self-conscious," she said. "Honestly, you're vainer than I am." She giggled and poked him in the ribs. Then she reached into her bag and pulled out a tape recorder.

"Okay, you remember this one, don't you? I'll say a word, and you repeat it into the tape recorder. Then I'll play it back, and you can hear exactly how it sounded. Ready?"

"No."

"Aw, come on, Mr. O'Connor. Where's your spirit? I'll tell you what, if you do this exercise just once, maybe we can think of some kind of treat for you–"

"I . . . said . . . *no!*" Spit flew out of his mouth and halfway across the room.

Ellen looked shocked.

"I think he's a little tired," I said. "Maybe that's enough for today."

"Well, okay. If you think so."

"I do," I said. "I'll tell my mom what happened."

"Okay. Goodbye, Mr. O'Connor. I'll see you next week."

Dad grunted. I walked Ellen to the door.

When I came back, Dad had flipped on the TV. It was that show where they ride around with real policemen and film what they do. They were stopping someone who had driven through a red light.

"Are you okay, Dad?"

He took a big breath and let it out slowly. He stared at the TV.

"Can I get you anything?"

He shook his head.

All of a sudden, a terrible crashing sound came from the TV. The guy who had gone through the red light had taken off after being pulled over, and the police had chased him. His car had flown off the road and smashed into a tree. I didn't want to watch, but I couldn't pull my eyes away. I was trembling, and tears were rolling down my face.

"Mol . . . ly? Molly!"

I dove into Dad's arms and started to cry. I couldn't stop sobbing. I made the wheelchair shake. He lifted his good hand and patted my hair.

"Ssshh . . . ssshhh . . . ssshhh . . . ," he said softly.

When I finally calmed down and looked up at him, there were tears in his eyes too.

"I'm sorry, Daddy. I'm so, so sorry."

"What . . . you . . . mean? Why . . . sorry?"

"It was my fault. I was being a jerk, and you were trying to cheer me up . . . and then I made you laugh, and you didn't see the car . . . and now sometimes you can't even look at me. . . ."

I started sobbing again.

"No . . . Molly . . . no."

He lifted my chin and looked into my eyes.

"Not . . . your . . . fault. I . . . don't . . . blame . . . you. It's . . . me . . . should . . . feel . . . guil-ty."

He had to struggle to get each word out. It was the most I'd heard him say since the accident.

"Guilty?" I asked. "What do you mean?"

"Can't . . . take . . . care . . . of . . . you."

I threw my arms around him.

"Dad, don't worry about that. I can take care of myself."

I wiped the tears off my face, and then off his.

The next morning, I was in the library writing in my journal when Chrys found me.

"Hey," he said, "I thought you were going to meet me outside class."

"Oh yeah. Sorry. I guess I forgot."

"That's not like you. You okay?"

"Yeah," I said. "I'm all right. I guess I'm just worried about my dad."

"What's up?"

"It's something he said last night. He said he feels guilty because he can't take care of me. I think he misses the same things I do. He misses the way

we were. I wrote something about it–do you want
to see?"

Chrys looked surprised. "Are you sure?"

"Yeah. It's okay. Go ahead."

He picked it up and read.

> I dreamed
> We were walking
>
> Sun on our faces
> Wind in our hair
>
> Tall and straight
> As trees
>
> And nothing
> Broken
>
> And nothing
> Between us
>
> But that was
> Just a dream

He handed it back to me.

"It's beautiful," he said. "And sad."

"The thing is," I said, "I know he's in there. I

can see it in his eyes. But it's like he's trapped. I wish I knew what to do."

"You'll think of something."

"Yeah. You're probably right. His birthday is coming up. Maybe I can think of something by then."

Chrys took out a thick, glossy book.

"What's that?" I asked.

"It's the TechnoSoft catalog. I got it from Mrs. Raptor. She said we could pick out our prize for making it into the final round. We each get two hundred and fifty dollars' worth of software."

"A lot of good *that*'ll do me. I don't even have a computer."

"Who knows? Maybe you'll get one."

"Yeah, right. I can't even get a new pair of shoes."

"But what if we win the grand prize? Then you'll have a brand-new laptop."

"Yeah, well, I'm not holding my breath or anything. There are a lot of other schools in the finals, and some of them are twice as big as Pine Ridge. We're going to have to beat some real hotshots. I'll tell you what—you can have my software too. You already have a computer."

"I can't do that. Come on, at least have a look. This catalog is unbelievable. There's stuff in here to make a computer do almost anything."

He was right, it was pretty amazing. I flipped through the book just out of curiosity, not looking for anything in particular. But then something caught my eye.

"Oh my God."

"What?" said Chrys. "What is it?"

"Oh my God. This is it. This is it *exactly*."

"This is *what*? What are you talking about?"

"Listen to this."

I read from the catalog.

CyberSpeak® is a revolutionary TechnoSoft product that lets your computer turn written words into human speech. Choose from a menu of preprogrammed voices or follow the easy instructions to record a voice of your own choosing. Tonal variation and inflection are remarkably similar to real speech.

You can generate speech from normal text

in standard word-processing formats, or you can use the special QuickSpeak® mode to select entire words or syllables with the click of a mouse. With practice, this feature allows conversion speeds that approach normal speaking fluency.

"You're right," said Chrys. "It's perfect. It's exactly what he needs."

"We have to win that contest," I said.

"Do you think our presentation is good enough?"

"I don't know. I'd feel better if we had more. Something to put us over the top, you know?"

"Is there time to change it?"

"I think so. We've got about three weeks."

"Three weeks?" Chrys's face went pale.

"What's wrong?"

"What day is the final round?" he asked.

"It's on a Tuesday. April tenth, I think."

He looked relieved.

"All right. That should be okay."

"Why? What's up?"

"I was going to tell you before," he said, "but I

didn't find out for sure until yesterday. We're moving. We leave around the middle of April."

"Leaving? Where? Why?"

"There's a doctor in Florida. He's a big-shot specialist in multisystem anomalies, whatever those are. My parents have been talking to him for months now. He thinks he may be able to help me, but it'll take a lot of tests, and maybe a lot of treatments. My parents think it's worth a try. They want him to start as soon as possible."

It took a while for his words to sink in. I was kind of stunned. I tried to think of something to say.

"Hey, congratulations. I mean . . . that's good news, right?"

"Yeah, I guess. I'll believe it when it happens. The doctors *always* think they can help—until they actually see me."

"But at least you're not leaving right away, right?"

"Right. I'll be here for the contest—and we're going to win."

"Thanks."

"After all," he said, "you have to stick by your friends."

16

On Dad's birthday, I came straight home from school. Mom met me at the door, kissed me, and hurried off to work. Dad was sitting in front of the TV watching a soap opera. I sat down on the floor beside him.

"Hey, Dad, would you mind if I turned off the TV?"

He looked at me.

"Wh . . . what . . . for?"

"I just wanted to show you something."

He clicked off the TV, and I took the remote. I

undid the brakes on his wheelchair and wheeled him across the room. Then I opened the closet and took out his jacket.

"What . . . you . . . do . . . ing?"

"It's a surprise, Dad. For your birthday. But we've got to go outside."

"What . . . sur . . . prise?"

"I can't tell you. But I know you'll like it. Please? It won't take long."

He frowned and looked anxiously at the door.

"Not . . . too . . . long," he said.

"I promise."

We rode down the elevator to the first floor. An older woman was standing there when the door opened. She looked startled. She glanced at my dad, then at me, and smiled nervously.

"Can I help you with the door?" she asked.

"That'd be great," I said.

Outside, it was a beautiful, sunny day. I stopped for a second and leaned over to check on Dad. He was blinking like a bear coming out of hibernation. I started pushing him down the sidewalk.

"It's not too far," I said. "We'll be there in a minute."

"Slow . . . down," he said.

●　　●　　●

When we reached the park, I went straight to a little flower bed that was tucked in a corner away from the main path. The air smelled like lilacs and roses. As we got closer, Chrys got up from a bench and walked over to meet us.

"Dad, this is my friend Chrys. He goes to my school. Chrys, this is my dad."

"Hi, Mr. O'Connor. Molly has told me a lot about you. It's nice to finally meet you."

Dad nodded.

"Is everything ready?" I asked.

"Yeah," said Chrys. "Over here by the bench. I think you were right. This is a good spot."

I wheeled my dad in front of the bench and set the brakes. Chrys took a small jar of nectar out of his pocket and unscrewed the cap. Then he took a deep breath and got really still.

Nothing happened for five or ten minutes. He looked frozen in place; you couldn't even tell he was breathing. Dad gave me a worried look. I patted his arm and smiled. Then it started to happen.

The first one was red and white. It flitted up from the garden bed and landed on Chrys's knee. The next was light green. It dropped down from the branches of a lilac tree. A big white one came out of nowhere and circled us twice before it landed on the back of Dad's chair.

They kept coming. Soon they were dancing and fluttering all around us in little swirls and waves. I looked over to check on my dad. His eyes were real big, and his face was tilted up toward the sky. But the best part was his mouth. If you didn't know him, you might have missed it, but I saw it right away. It was twisted, but it was a smile. It was definitely a smile.

17

On the way home, we walked in the sunshine. I noticed that Dad had his eyes closed.

"Is it too bright?" I asked.

"No. Feels . . . good."

I remembered a song he used to sing for me about the sun. I sang it. When I finished, he wanted more, so I kept singing all the way home. I even sang in the elevator on the way up to our floor. But when we got to our apartment, I stopped.

The door was open, and I could hear Mom on the phone in the kitchen. She was shouting.

"Please listen to what I'm saying. . . . Well, why not? You're the police—isn't that your job? . . . Why does it matter how long? They're gone! . . . No, you don't understand—there's nowhere else they'd go. . . . Stop telling me to calm down! . . . Fine! I'll go out and look for them myself."

She slammed down the phone, and then she saw us.

"Where in the name of God have you been?"

"We . . . we just went out," I said. "To the park."

"To the *park*? Do you have any idea what I've been going through?"

"But Mom, we weren't gone that long. You weren't even supposed to be home yet."

"I called, damn it! I called, and when no one answered, I drove here like a maniac. I left right in the middle of work, for God's sake! I don't even know if I have a job anymore."

"Mom, I'm sorry. I didn't think—"

"That's right, you didn't. All you ever think about is yourself. *You* want new shoes. *You* want to go to a different school. Well, right now, you can just go to your room. You can come out when you've learned to think about someone else for a change."

"But Mom—"

"Just go! Get out of my sight!"

I walked into my room and shut the door.

●   ●   ●

I couldn't sleep that night. I lay in bed, listening to the sounds in the apartment—creaky beams and clanging pipes. Around midnight, Mom came out of her bedroom and went into the kitchen. I heard her boil some water and pull a chair up to the table. Then I heard a funny sound. I couldn't figure out what it was. I got up and walked down the hall in my bare feet.

She was sitting at the table with a cup of tea in front of her. She was holding up a mirror with one hand and cutting her bangs with the other. That's what I'd heard. It was the sound of the scissors.

I went to the fridge and poured myself a glass of milk, then sat down across from her. I started to say something, but I stopped. For some reason, I thought of what Chrys had said.

Sometimes nothing is the best thing to do.

For a long time, the only sound was the *snip, snip, snip* of the scissors. Then, in a low voice, without looking up at me, she started to talk.

"You know when the last time was I got my hair done?" she said. "It was the day of the accident."

She kept working the scissors, snipping after every few words.

"Your dad and I were supposed to go to a party at the Mitchells' that night. He took you to your game while I went out to buy a dress and get my hair done. It was supposed to be a treat.

"I found something on sale that I really liked. I wanted to show it off, but when I got home, you and your dad weren't there. I put the dress on so I could surprise you when you got home.

"I remember singing that song from *West Side Story*–"I Feel Pretty." I was dancing around in front of the mirror like an idiot. Then I saw the light flashing on the answering machine.

"A stranger's voice said there'd been an accident. It was someone calling from the hospital. When I called back, it took forever to get someone who could tell me anything. They kept putting me on hold. When I finally spoke to the doctor, he said your dad was in surgery. He said I couldn't talk to you, either–you were unconscious.

"It's a miracle I made it to the hospital in one piece. I don't even remember driving. When I got there, your dad was still in surgery. You were still unconscious. Your neck was in a brace, and your leg was strapped to a board. Your face was all puffy and covered with dried blood. They'd put tubes in your arms and in your nose.

"I stayed with you until they took you off to surgery too. I wouldn't let go of you. The nurse had to pull my arms away."

Mom took one last look in the mirror and put it down. She laid the scissors on top of it and looked at me. Big tears rolled down her face. I had never seen her cry.

"When I came home today and you two weren't here . . . it felt like the day of the accident . . . all over again."

I got up, walked around the table, and climbed into her lap like I hadn't done for years. I put my arms around her neck and held her as tightly as I could.

18

The menu board at the front of the cafeteria line said TUNA SURPRISE.

"What's the surprise?" I asked.

"Vy I should tell you?" said Mrs. Grywzinsky. "Is surprise."

"What if I were allergic or something?"

"You tell me vat you allergic to. I tell you if it kill you."

She grinned. There were little brown spots between her teeth. She scooped up a big spoonful of Tuna Surprise and held it over my tray. It slid off the spoon with a sucking noise and splatted on my plate. I covered it with a napkin so it wouldn't contaminate anything else.

Chrys wasn't sitting in his usual corner. I sat down at the empty table and looked at my lunch. The fruit salad was the only thing I was brave enough to eat. After that, I pushed the rest away and took out my journal. But before I started to write, Chrys came running up and flopped down in the chair next to me. He was out of breath.

"What's up?" I asked. "Why are you panting like a dog?"

"I've got it!"

"Dog breath?"

"I'm serious. I've got an idea for our presentation. I think it's the one that puts us over the top."

"Let's hear it."

He rummaged around in his backpack and pulled out a small book.

"I was at the downtown library all morning. Mrs. Raptor gave me a pass for my other classes. That place is so cool. I was looking through the zoology section, and I found this."

The book was called *Lepidoptera: Miracles of Adaptation*. He opened it to a page he had marked and started to read.

> *"In reality, the brilliant blue found in some butterfly wings is not their true color. The wings contain no blue pigment of any kind. Instead, they are covered with millions upon millions of tiny iridescent scales. It is the elegant structure and arrangement of these scales that produces their intense, shimmering color."*

There were a bunch of diagrams, too, and lots of color photos.

"That's not all," he said. "After I found that chapter, I got on the Internet and found this."

He showed me a printout of a Web page for a butterfly farm in Costa Rica.

"We can order a pupa, and they'll send it by airmail in a couple of days. After that, it takes one or two weeks for the butterfly to emerge. We can order an iridescent species and use it to illustrate the new part of our presentation. What do you think?"

"It's brilliant," I said. "What kind should we get?"

He smiled and flipped the textbook to another marked page.

"This one."

It was a photograph of a butterfly called a Blue Morpho. It was huge—probably six or seven inches across—and its wings shimmered with purples and blues. Exactly like Chrys's.

I picked up the printout. There was a price list. The Blue Morpho pupae were expensive.

"Don't worry," said Chrys, "I've got some money saved. I can pay my mom, and she can order it with her credit card. I'll pay your half too."

"I don't know when I can pay you back."

"Don't sweat it," he said. "When we win, it'll be more than worth it."

"Are you sure your mom will order it for us?"

"She won't mind," he said. "It's a school thing. And besides, she's crazy about you. If she knows it's for our project, she'll help us for sure."

"That reminds me," I said. I leaned closer and whispered, "Do your parents know that I know? About your wings?"

"No," he whispered back. "I didn't tell them. I

thought it might freak them out. They're always afraid that if word got around, everyone would treat me like a monster or something."

"Yeah, but sooner or later, it's bound to happen. I mean, let's face it, you might be like this for the rest of your life. You can't hide under that overcoat forever."

"I guess they're hoping someone will fix me."

With our heads huddled together, we didn't notice J.T. sneaking up behind us.

"Well, look at you two—all lovey-dovey. Too busy smooching to eat lunch?"

"I *was* hungry until I saw *you*," I said. "Now I want to vomit."

"What did I tell you about that big mouth of yours? One of these days I'm gonna shut your face for good."

"Go ahead," I said. "Why don't you prove what a big man you are by fighting a girl right in the middle of the cafeteria? I'd like that."

"Yeah?" he said. "Let's see how you like *this*."

He grabbed something off the table and took off across the lunchroom. He was out the door before I realized what he'd taken. It was my journal.

When I caught up to him, he was standing in

the hallway next to Courtney and Vanessa. He had the journal open, and he was reading out loud.

"*I dreamed we were walking.* Isn't that romantic? It's a poem about her little dreamboat."

"Give it back, J.T.!"

"What's the matter? Don't you want to be a famous writer like your daddy? I was just sharing your masterpiece. I especially like the love letter to your boyfriend."

I lunged for it, but he held it over his head and used his other hand to push me away.

"*Sun on our faces. Wind in our hair.* Hey, this is *so* poetic. It's like Shakespeare or something. You really *should* be famous. I'm gonna make copies and hand them out all over school."

I jumped up and knocked the journal out of his hand, but before I could grab it, he kicked it down the hall. We both ran after it, but someone else got there before we did. Someone in bright red high-heeled shoes.

"What's this?" asked Miss Gruber.

"It's mine," we both said at once.

She picked it up and read the front cover.

"Property of Molly O'Connor." She raised an eye-

brow and looked at J.T. "Well, Julius, either you've changed your name, or you're mistaken. You haven't changed your name, have you?"

J.T. turned red and slunk down the hall. Miss Gruber handed me my journal.

"Thanks," I said.

"That's okay, honey. The pleasure's all mine. It's hard to believe that little monster is really Bobby Jenkins's son. He must get it from his mother."

"You know his dad?" I asked. "The congressman?"

"I used to. I knew him back when we were both about your age."

"Really? What was he like? Was he a big deal back then, too?"

"Are you kidding? He was a zit-faced little wimp. Hardly said a word to anyone. Everybody made fun of him. Like father, like son."

"What do you mean?"

"J.T. wasn't always J.T., you know. They used to call him Little Julie, and a few names worse than that. He was small for his age, and he had learning problems. They had to hold him back—twice. He took a lot of teasing for that. Until he grew ten inches in one summer. That's when the teasing stopped."

"If he knows what it's like being picked on, why does he do it?"

"That's how it is when people get hurt," she said. "Some find a way to rise above it. Others, like Julius, just hold it inside, and it grows there like a weed."

She looked down the hallway, where J.T. was already pushing around some other kid.

"So, how well did you know his dad?"

"Actually," she said, "we were best friends."

19

Chrys was right. His mom was happy to order the Blue Morpho for us, and we bought two, just to be safe. We were cutting it close, though—the competition was only two weeks away.

They arrived on a Saturday. Chrys called to tell me, and I ran all the way to his house without stopping.

"I waited for you so we could open them together," he said. He was holding a small cardboard box with a few airholes in each side. He pulled off the packing tape and opened it carefully.

Two perfect little pupae lay nestled in a bed of straw, each one attached to a twig. They were pale green and shiny and shaped like little birds' eggs.

"Wow," I said. "They're incredible. I've never seen a real chrysalis before."

"I never told you," said Chrys. "But that's why my name is spelled so funny. It's short for Chrysalis."

"Really? That's a beautiful name."

"I hate it," he said. "I always wanted a normal name."

"Well, I think normal is way overrated."

"Maybe," he said. "I wouldn't know."

He put the twig and the pupae inside an old glass aquarium.

"What do we do now?" I asked.

He smiled.

"Nothing."

●　　●　　●

That afternoon, I asked Mom if I could take Dad back to the park. She said okay, as long as we weren't gone too long. On the way there, he was more relaxed than the first time. We went to the same little garden as before, and I parked his chair where he could sit in the sun.

While we were sitting there, a little kid came up and started talking to us. He couldn't have been more than three or four.

"Whatcha doin'?" he asked.

"We're just sitting here," I said.

"Who's he?" He pointed at Dad.

"That's my father."

"He looks funny."

I glanced at Dad to see his reaction, but he didn't seem to mind. The kid walked over and put his hand on the wheelchair.

"Why does your chair have wheels?"

"It's . . . a . . . race . . . car."

The kid laughed. I'm not sure if he got the joke or if it was just my dad's voice, but he thought something was hilarious. He giggled so much, it made *me* laugh. Then Dad started laughing too. That's when the trouble started.

Maybe it was the way Dad's mouth got all crooked and twisty, or maybe it was the weird whooping sound he made when he laughed. Whatever it was, the kid suddenly stopped laughing. He looked scared and started to cry. Dad tried to stop laughing, but that just made him cough and choke. His face turned red, and his eyes bugged out. He reached for the arm of his wheelchair to steady himself, but he grabbed the kid's hand instead. That freaked the little guy out. He started screaming at the top of his lungs.

Dad let go of him right away, but he kept on screaming. Then, out of nowhere, a tall woman in nice clothes swooped down and grabbed him up. Dad tried to say something, but he couldn't stop coughing. The woman looked at him like he was some kind of monster. She squeezed the kid to her chest and hurried away.

"Mommy," wailed the kid, "he scared me!"

"Stay away from that man," she said. "He's sick. You don't want to get sick too."

When Dad got his breath back, he made me take him home. He didn't say a word for the rest of the day.

20

Two days before the competition, Chrys called me.

"Hurry," he said. "They're coming."

When I got there, one of the Blue Morphos was already out. It was perched on the twig, and its wings were all shriveled up like little prunes. The other one was just beginning to appear. We knelt on the floor and pressed our noses against the glass.

"You were kind of quiet in school today," said Chrys.

"Yeah," I said. "It's my dad again."

I told him what had happened in the park.

"He's just as bad as he was before," I said. "Maybe worse. He doesn't want to go out anymore. He just sits there, and the TV isn't even on. I don't know what to do."

The first butterfly was moving its wings now. It opened and closed them slowly, and they began to unfold.

"This probably isn't the best time to tell you," said Chrys, "but it's official. We leave for Florida on Wednesday."

"You made your parents wait until after the competition, didn't you?"

"Yeah, kind of," he said. "It wasn't a big deal."

"Thanks."

"I'm not sure how I feel about it," he said. "About leaving, I mean."

"Yeah?"

"I'm not sure if I should be excited or scared."

"Who says you can't be both?"

Now the second butterfly was out too. The first one's wings were completely open; they looked like blue satin. The two empty shells still hung from their twigs.

"I wish people were like that," I said.

"Like what?"

"I wish we could just change everything all at once—hide away for a while, and then come back as something completely new."

"Yeah," he said. "I know what you mean."

21

"**You know how** much I want to be there, don't you?" said Mom. She pulled her coat on and dug her keys out of her purse. "I tried to switch shifts with Charlene, but her little boy is sick. Do you forgive me?"

"It's okay, Mom. Don't worry about it."

"Well, promise me you'll tell me all about it tonight."

"I will," I said. "I promise."

She stepped back and looked me over from head to toe. Then she frowned.

"What's wrong?" I asked. "Don't I look okay?"

"You look beautiful. But something's missing. . . . I know—after I leave, look under the kitchen table. There's a bag there for you." She smiled.

"What?" I said. "What is it?"

"You'll see." She kissed me on the forehead and held my face in her hands. "Molly, I'm so proud of you. Do you know that? Even when I forget to tell you?"

"Yeah," I said. "I know."

As soon as she left, I ran to the kitchen and pulled out the bag. Inside was a brand-new pair of shoes.

● ● ●

Even though the contest was for the whole city, the finals were held at our school. There were ten teams, and each one had to go up onstage by themselves and give their presentation. The order was decided by drawing numbers. Chrys and I ended up with the last spot. That gave us lots of time to stand around being nervous. I felt sick.

We waited outside with the other teams at the back door to the auditorium. Our models and the aquarium with the Blue Morphos were stacked up on a metal cart we had borrowed from Mrs. Raptor. Chrys's parents were there fussing over him.

"Ow! Stop that!" He jerked away from his mom, who was trying to brush his hair.

"I forgot to bring some nectar," she said. "Should we go back to the house and get it?"

"Leave the boy alone," said Mr. Lepido. "He's fine." He had a video camera. He was filming Chrys getting brushed.

"Just drink some water before you go on," said Mrs. Lepido. "You don't want to get dehydrated under those lights."

"Mom, that's enough," said Chrys. "And Dad, would you please turn that thing off? Why don't you guys go get some seats?"

"We already did," said Mrs. Lepido. "We have two seats saved right in the front row. Don't forget to wave. Daddy will be filming."

"Listen," said Chrys, "you guys have to go now. Molly and I need to go over a few things. We have to concentrate."

"All right, dear," said Mrs. Lepido with one last swipe of her brush. "Good luck. You too, Molly. And don't forget to smile."

When they finally left, Chrys breathed a huge sigh of relief.

"Jeez," he said, "I thought they'd never go. How do you feel?"

"Like throwing up. Do we really have anything else to go over?"

"Yeah. We need to figure out how I'm going to ride all the way to Florida with them without going nuts."

"Aw, come on. They're sweet. It's great that they're here. You're lucky."

"Yeah," he said. "I guess. How about you? Is your mom coming?"

"No. She had to work. She's not much help at stuff like this, anyway. She gets so tense it just makes me more nervous. Dad was the one who always knew how to calm me down. He used to come to everything—spelling bees, softball games, piano recitals—anything I did. He'd always sit where he knew I'd see him. Then, when he caught my eye, he'd flash me a big, goofy smile and give me the thumbs-up sign. It was kind of stupid, but it worked. I always felt better. I wish he were here."

"Did you ask him?"

"Are you kidding?" I said. "I can't even get him to leave the apartment. There's no way he's going to come here and sit in an auditorium full of people."

"Maybe," said Chrys. "But just because he wouldn't do it for himself doesn't mean he wouldn't do it for you."

I hadn't thought of that.

"Do you really think so?" I asked.

"Well," he said, "there's one way to find out."

● ● ●

I ran all the way home. It was only a few blocks, but by the time I got there and ran up the stairs, I was so out of breath I could hardly talk. When I burst in on Dad, I scared him.

"Don't worry," I said. "It's okay."

It took me a minute to catch my breath.

"Dad, I need you to do something for me. It might be hard, but I wouldn't ask unless I really needed you."

He looked straight into my eyes.

"Any . . . thing," he said.

22

We must have been a strange sight—me, Dad, and the wheelchair flying down the sidewalk like some crazy event in the Special Olympics. When we got to school, I wheeled him into the auditorium. It was packed.

Everyone turned and stared as I pushed Dad down the aisle. When I got to the front row, I spotted Mr. and Mrs. Lepido.

"These are Chrys's parents," I said. "Mr. and Mrs. Lepido, this is my dad. Would you mind if he sat next to you?"

"No, of course not," said Mr. Lepido. "Put him right here."

"Thank you. I have to go. Chrys and I still have to get ready."

I ran back up the aisle and out the door. By the time I got to the backstage entrance, Chrys was almost ready to go on.

"There you are," he said. "I was beginning to worry. Is your dad here?"

"Yeah," I said. "I left him next to your parents in the front row."

Someone behind me started laughing. It was J.T. He had followed me from the auditorium.

"Did I hear you right?" he said. "Was that cripple really your father? Now I know why you're in love with Freak-Boy. Next to your old man, even *he* looks good."

"Why don't you shut your face?" I said.

"At least I've *got* one. Your dad's face looks like it's about to fall off. He was drooling! I was right—he really *is* a retard!"

I turned around and looked him in the eye.

"Why do you use that word so much?" I asked. "Is that what they used to call you? Little Julie Retard?"

For just a second, I saw a look in his eyes like a hurt little boy's. But then he got angry. Before I could stop him, he grabbed my arm and twisted it behind my back.

"Leave her alone!" yelled Chrys.

J.T. ignored him. I tried to get loose, but he yanked my arm even harder.

"Ow!" I said. "You're hurting me!"

Then, all of a sudden, he let go.

When I turned around, Chrys was clinging to his back and riding him like a horse. J.T. tried to pull him off, but he wouldn't let go, even when J.T. lunged backward and slammed him into the wall. He tried to flip Chrys over his shoulder, but that didn't work either. All it did was throw him off balance. He stumbled for a second, and then they both toppled over and landed on our cart.

The aquarium crashed to the ground, and glass flew everywhere. Chrys sliced up his arm when he tried to break his fall, and the models were smashed under J.T.'s weight. But the two Blue Morphos weren't hurt. They fluttered above our heads for a second, then flew off into the sky.

When J.T. saw the blood running down Chrys's

arm, he got scared and ran. Chrys took a piece of cloth from the broken butterfly model and used it to wrap up his cut. Inside, people were clapping. The team before us was done.

"Come on," said Chrys. "We're on."

"What are you talking about?" I said. "Look at you. You're hurt."

"I'm fine," he said. "Let's go."

"But the morphos are gone," I said. "And the models . . . they're ruined. What are we going to present?"

"Come on," he said. "It's now or never."

●　●　●

When we walked onstage, I was still dazed.

"Are you ready?" said Chrys.

"I don't know what to do," I whispered.

"Just do it like we rehearsed," said Chrys.

I turned toward the audience and spotted Chrys's parents. They were wringing their hands and nodding encouragement. But it was my dad who got me to settle down. He was looking up at me with a big, crooked grin, and his good hand was resting on his leg with the thumb pointing up.

I took a deep breath and began.

"'Metamorphosis and Iridescence in Butterflies,' by Molly O'Connor and Chrys Lepido."

Suddenly, a gasp went through the audience. People were staring up at us with open mouths. I looked back at Chrys to see what was wrong.

He had turned his back to the audience. His overcoat lay in a pile at his feet. Under the spotlight, shining and shimmering for everyone to see, were his beautiful wings.

"Go ahead," he whispered. "Just like we rehearsed."

"The blue that you are now seeing in these butterflies' . . . in Chrys's wings . . . is not a true blue, like the color of a blue flower or a blue car. . . ."

I pointed to Chrys, and my hand brushed the edge of his wing. A little puff of blue powder swirled in the light. It sparkled all the way down to the stage.

23

The next day, I ran to Chrys's house as soon as school was over. His dad was out front, loading boxes into a trailer.

"Hi, Molly," he said. "Chrys is upstairs. I think he's expecting you. He wanted to tell you something before we leave."

I ran up the stairs and into his room. It was completely empty, except for a few thumbtacks on the wall and the big hook on the ceiling where his sleeping bag had been. I pushed open the window and stepped out onto the roof.

He was sitting in the sunshine, looking toward the mountains. A big monarch was sunning itself on his shoulder, and another was fluttering around his head. Chrys's wings opened and closed slowly, rippling with little waves of purple and blue.

"Hey," I said. "Isn't that Chrys Lepido, winner of the TechnoSoft science competition?"

He turned around and smiled.

"Yeah. Do you want my autograph?"

"No way," I said. "*I'm* famous too." I sat down next to him.

"So what was it like today?" he asked. "Was the whole school talking about me?"

"Pretty much," I said.

"I'm sorry you had to deal with it by yourself. I thought about coming in, but I was chicken. Besides, I had to pack up my room."

"That's okay," I said. "It wasn't as bad as I expected. People were mostly just curious. I sure was the center of attention, though."

"I'll bet Vanessa didn't like *that*."

We both laughed.

"What about J.T.?" asked Chrys. "Didn't *he* give you a hard time?"

"He wasn't there. Mr. Dinkerman suspended him."

Chrys's jaw dropped. "You're kidding!"

"I'm serious. Miss Gruber told me he may not come back. She didn't say so, but I think she had something to do with it. She talked to J.T.'s father, and he's thinking about pulling J.T. out of Pine Ridge and putting him in a new school. One with more *structure,* she said."

"How about one with guards and handcuffs?" said Chrys. We laughed again.

Behind Chrys's yard, a steep hill dropped off into a valley covered with farmland. A little creek ran through it, sparkling like a silver thread.

"Your dad said you wanted to tell me something."

"Yeah," said Chrys. "I just wanted to warn you— you might not get rid of me as easily as you thought."

"What do you mean?"

"We're coming back."

At first I didn't get it.

"But . . . but what about the house? And all your things . . ."

"Most of our stuff is in storage. We're renting

the house instead of selling it. We'll be in Florida until the end of summer, but we'll be back by the first day of school."

"Chrys, that's fantastic!" I wanted to hug him, but I wasn't sure how to do it with his wings. "But how? What happened?"

"I told my parents I wanted to stay. I told them it was more important to me than getting rid of my wings. We're just going down there for the initial tests. If they look good, I'll probably have the treatments next summer."

"I can't believe it," I said. "I was all sad about saying goodbye, and now you're coming back."

"Yep. Wings and all."

"What's that going to be like for you?" I asked.

"I don't know," he said. "But at least it's not a secret anymore. Maybe the hardest part is over."

"Well," I said, "I guess we can figure it out in September."

"Yeah," he said. "We can figure it out together."

I stood up and stretched my legs.

"I have to go," I said. "I promised my dad I'd take him to the park."

"Tell him I said hi."

"I will. And don't forget to write, okay? Even if it's just a stupid postcard or something."

"Okay."

I climbed back up to Chrys's window. When I got there, I stopped and turned around.

"Hey," I said.

"Yeah?"

"I wanted to thank you for what you did last night. I've been thinking about it a lot. If it were me, I don't know if I could have done the same thing."

He laughed. "That's because you're not a giant mutant insect thing."

"No, I'm serious. You know what I mean. I would have wanted to, but I don't know if I actually could have done it."

He looked at me and thought about it.

"Yeah," he said. "You would have. You would have done the exact same thing."

"Why are you so sure?"

"Because I know you," he said. "That's how you are."

"How?" I asked.

"True blue."

24

"All right," said Mrs. Raptor, "everyone please settle down. We'll be starting in a minute."

I made sure the speakers were hooked up, and I adjusted Dad's laptop so his good hand could reach it.

"Are you ready?" I whispered.

He nodded.

It had taken him a while to figure out the new software, but he worked hard at it, and he kept getting better every day. The program wasn't as fast as they said in the catalog, but it wasn't bad. It only took a few seconds to put together a sentence, and we even found a way to use it with other programs. He wasn't just talking with it; he was starting to write again.

At first, we used the voice that came with the program. That was a little too weird. It made him sound like some guy on a TV commercial. Luckily, Mom found a recording of an interview Dad did for a radio show, and we used bits and pieces of it to put his own voice into the computer. Well, it wasn't *exactly* his voice. It was more like a robot doing an imitation of him. That's how he decided what to name his computer. He called it Robo-Rick.

Once I got everything hooked up, I went back to my desk and sat down.

"All right, class," said Mrs. Raptor. "As you all know, Molly's father has generously agreed to speak to us about his work as a science writer. I gave him the list of questions you submitted last week, and he has prepared answers for all of them. We'll have some time for spontaneous discussion at the end.

"Here's the first question: 'I think I want to be a writer someday, but how do I know if I have anything worth saying?'"

The room went quiet. Dad pressed a few keys on his laptop, and Robo-Rick started to talk.

"Everyone has something to say," he said. "The hard part is finding the courage to say it."

Dad looked at me and grinned a crooked grin.

I smiled back and gave him two thumbs up.

ABOUT THE AUTHOR

Jeffrey Lee writes fiction and nonfiction for children and adults. He lives with his wife and their two daughters in Seattle, where he has worked as a family physician for more than sixteen years.

His next book, *Catch a Fish, Throw a Ball, Ride a Bike* (Three Rivers Press, 2004), will help parents instruct their kids in the life skills that every child should learn.